SANTA'S COUNTDOWN TO CHRISTMAS

24 DAYS OF STORIES

By **Kim Thompson**
Illustrated by **Élodie Duhameau**

CRACKBOOM!

TODAY IS
DECEMBER
1

Santa Claus has gathered all the elves in the toy workshop for a big meeting. Christmas is coming, and they have exactly twenty-four days to get ready.

"That's not much time!" says a little elf named Snippet.

Santa smiles. "It's enough. We're always ready by Christmas Eve."

But the elves are worried. Every year there are more and more children, and more and more toys to make. Can they do it?

"We can do it," says Santa. "I can feel it right down to my toes." Santa wiggles his toes inside his boots.

"Can you feel it, too?"

All the elves wiggle their toes. "Yes," they answer.

"Pardon me? I can't hear you," says Santa.

"Can we do it?"

"YES!" The elves shout so loudly the windows rattle. Santa grins.

Sprig and Twig hand out the work assignments. Mrs. Claus has something for Santa, too: a list of everything he has to do before Christmas. Santa looks at the long, long, looooong paper.

"*Jumpin' jingle bells!*" he says. "I'd better get busy!"

It's time to check the sleigh.
Forge the mechanic says it's in fine shape. All it needs is a good cleaning and a fresh coat of paint.
Santa thinks there must be mice in the garage.
They've been chewing on the seat cushions!
The tailor elves will have to fix those up.

Tek is looking over the sleigh, too. He's the elf who invents things, and he thinks the sleigh needs more gadgets.
"I can put in a GPS," says Tek.
"What's GPS? Is it like a BLT?" asks Santa, suddenly feeling hungry.
"No!" laughs Tek. "It's not a sandwich. It's a computer map that shows you where you are."
"That will be very useful on Christmas Eve," says Mrs. Claus.
"Not as useful as a sandwich," grumbles Santa.

This is the day that Santa goes to the post office in the village to pick up his mail. Children all around the world have written to him, so there are lots and lots of letters! Santa needs a little help getting them all back to the workshop. They load up the sled and start off down the road.

"There are an awful, awful lot of letters here," says Sprig. "Hundreds!"

"Thousands!" says Twig.

"MILLIONS!" says Sprig.

Santa laughs. "That's right, and we're going to read each and every one."

Suddenly they hear shouting and a loud whoosh as something goes zooming past them. It's Tek on his new invention: a rocket-powered sled!

"*Leapin' lollipops!*" says Santa. "That doesn't look very safe."

"Tek is a very clever elf, but he sometimes forgets things," sighs Mrs. Claus. "Like seatbelts and *brakes*!"

Santa notices they have an unexpected passenger. "That puppy again! He's been following us for days. Should we adopt him, Mrs. Claus?"

Mrs. Claus smiles. "I think he's already decided to adopt us."

Santa and Mrs. Claus spend the whole day reading letters from children. There are so many letters to read that they will have to stay up late. It's a lot of work, but this is a job they really enjoy. They especially love the drawings they receive, and always put them up on the wall.

As they read, they tell Sprig what toys are needed, and Sprig writes them down.

"Here's a request for a Sleepy Baby Panda," says Mrs. Claus.

"That's our most popular toy. Everybody wants one!" says Sprig.

Twig is reading emails from children on the computer. "Another soccer ball and a ukulele!" Sprig adds them to the list.

"*Jumpin' gingerbread!*" says Santa, holding up a letter. "This young fellow named Ali just moved to a new town. He hasn't made any new friends yet and he's very lonely."

"Oh, the poor boy," says Mrs. Claus. "Maybe a nice present will cheer him up."

"That's the problem!" exclaims Santa. "He wants me to bring a book about penguins for his sister, but he doesn't want anything for himself."

"Penguin book." Sprig writes it down.

"I'm going to think of something to give to Ali," says Santa. "Something extra, extra special."

This is the day the elves start making toys. Everyone is excited and ready to go. Sprig has the list of all the toys the children asked for in thcir letters, and Tek has a special new invention to show them.

"What is it?" asks Santa. "Some kind of TV?"

"No, it's Tek's Terrific Toy Tabulator. It tells us how many toys we need to make!" Tek pushes a button. Lights flash, and the machine goes *sproing* and *boing* and *kerpopple* and *fzzzitz*! Then the screen lights up with a very big number indeed.

"*Sufferin' snowflakes!*" says Santa.

Everyone stares at the screen. Nobody says a word.

Then Santa speaks up.

"Do not panic, friends! We can do it, I know we can."

The elves nod and grin.

"Man your stations!" calls Santa. "Let the toy-making begin!"

Soon the room is buzzing with activity.

Snippet whispers in Santa's ear. "That's the biggest number I've ever seen in my whole entire life."

"Me, too," says Santa.

On Santa's list for today is a fitness test, which he is not looking forward to. Spark is Santa's trainer elf, and it is his job to make sure Santa is in shape for Christmas Eve.

He begins with a strength test. Santa grabs a sack full of toys, but it's so heavy he can't even lift it off the ground. "What's in here, bricks?" he asks.

"No good," says Spark. "We need to build up those muscles."

Next Santa has to climb up and down the chimney as many times as he can. He is huffing and puffing after just two trips.

Spark frowns. "Your cardio needs work, too. What have you been doing all year, Santa?"

"Taking naps," says Santa with a sigh.

The final test is for balance. Spark tells him to walk along the peak of the roof. "*Easy peasy!*" says Santa. He takes a few steps. He starts to wobble. Then his feet slip and he slides right off the roof. Luckily Rudolph is there to catch him.

"Thanks, buddy," says Santa.

"Yoga will help your balance," says Spark. "Here's your training plan, Santa: running, climbing, weightlifting and yoga every morning, starting tomorrow."

"*Hollerin' hoptoads!*" says Santa. "And I was planning to sleep in tomorrow!"

Santa begins his training with Spark today.
It's not easy, but he is doing his best.

First he runs a long, long way, until his feet ache
and he can barely breathe.
"Doesn't this feel good?" asks Spark.
Santa just groans.

Then he tries the climbing wall.
"Keep going!" calls Spark.
"Climb to the top and ring the bell!"
"Yikes!" says Santa.

Next is weight training.
"We'll start with a light weight,"
says Spark.

The workout cnds with some yoga.
"This is the Tree Pose," says Spark.
"Stand on one foot, tall like a tree."
"I would be a much better tree
on two feet," says Santa.

Finally they are finished.
"At last!" says Santa. "I could sleep for a week."
"We'll do it all again tomorrow, bright and early," says Spark.
"*Gallopin' gumdrops!*" says Santa.

TODAY IS
DECEMBER
8

Santa and Mrs. Claus visit Tek in his workshop. He's got a lot of new inventions to show them. First is the GPS for Santa's sleigh.

"You will be able to see where you are at all times. That blinking yellow dot is you," explains Tek.

"Wonderful!" says Mrs. Claus.

"Can I be a red dot instead?" asks Santa.

Next Tek shows them a Flying Tea Service and a Robot Chicken.

"I'm not sure I really need those," says Santa.

Tek's final surprise for Santa is a pair of Laser Boots. "They detect icy patches and melt them with lasers."

"Lasers? Is that safe?" asks Mrs. Claus in surprise.

"My toes get pretty frosty on Christmas Eve," says Santa. "Are these boots warm?"

"Not really, but they can keep track of how many steps you take," says Tek.

Santa looks down. "*Blazin' booties!* They're warming up now!"

"Oops. They need a little more work," sighs Tek.

Santa thinks he'd rather stick with his old boots.

The next duty on Santa's list is to check on the Pet Room.
The elf in charge here is named Chortle.
"Welcome to my zoo!" says Chortle. The place is very noisy and wild.
"*Bouncin' baby baboons!*" says Santa.

"I'm afraid we don't have any of those, but we've got just about everything else," says Chortle. She shows Santa and Mrs. Claus around. Chortle can remember all the animals' names, even the twenty-seven mice. She introduces them to Merkle the hedgehog, Elsie the pig and a monkey named Chester who just loves to comb people's hair.

"Have you got all the pets we need?" asks Mrs. Claus.

Chortle nods. "Every single one!"

"Excellent," says Santa. "Thank you very much, Chester. I love my new hairdo. You should work in a barbershop."

On Santa's list for today is a visit to the Stuffed Animal Lab. This is where all the stuffed animals are hug-tested.

"We score them for softness and huggability," explains Poppy. "Sometimes we have to send them back to the workshop for more stuffing."

Mrs. Claus tries out a Sleepy Baby Panda Bear. She gives it ten out of ten for softness. And for huggability, eleven!

"We don't go higher than ten," laughs Poppy.

Two other elves are hug-testing, and one of them gives Puppy a perfect score!

Mrs. Claus looks around. Where did Santa go?

"There he is!" says Poppy. "And he's fast asleep!"

"Come on, sleeping beauty," says Mrs. Claus, waking him up.

"*Hoppin' holly!*" says Santa with a yawn. "I was just doing a nap test. This whole pile gets ten out of ten."

"I'm going to inspect the kitchen," announces Santa.
Mrs. Claus is surprised. "That's not on the list," she says.
"I'm putting it on the list," says Santa. "The baking must be tested!"
In the kitchen they find Ember and all her helpers hard at work.
"Mmm, I smell ginger," says Santa.
"The Swedish gingerbread cookies are in the oven. We're decorating
the shortbread right now," explains Ember.

She shows Santa the other goodies they've been
making: Italian struffoli, Polish angel wings, Austrian
raspberry linzer and Chinese almond cookies.
"I'd better taste a few," says Santa. "To make sure they're all right."
"Just don't eat them all!" laughs Ember. "When we finish all the cookies,
we'll start on the bread, pies and cakes."
"*Bust my buttons!*" says Santa. "I'll be back on cake day."

It's a bright, beautiful day. Chortle and Santa are taking the reindeer out for some exercise. The reindeer are very excited to be out in the sunshine. They chase each other and show off with loop-the-loops.

Santa isn't used to riding like this. He's getting very dizzy. "Please, Rudolph! No more loops!"

Next the reindeer play tag, and Rudolph is it.

"*Gallopin' gravy!*" calls Santa. "Don't you know any slower reindeer games? Like tic-tac-toe? Or chess?"

The reindeer race around for a whole hour before Cupid spots a lovely field of moss below. "Good. Let's go down. I'm starving," says Chortle.

Santa looks down at the moss. "Um, I'm not that hungry," he says.

Chortle laughs. "Don't worry, Santa. We don't have to eat moss. That's for the reindeer. Ember packed a nice lunch for us to eat."

"Phew!" says Santa.

Santa is excited about today's plans. It's finally time to travel around visiting children. Forge has repainted the sleigh, and the cushions have been repaired. The reindeer are keen and ready to fly.

Tek comes along for the ride with some new inventions to help out.

"I've got an Automatic Hand Shaker," says Tek. "And the Robot Chicken can talk to the children for you."

"But I like shaking hands and talking! I don't need any gadgets for that," says Santa in surprise.

"How about a Solar-Powered Hot Chocolate-Making Hat then?"

Santa smiles. "Now you're talking!"

At their first stop, they are greeted by a crowd of excited children, all cheering loudly. "*Cracklin' candy canes!*" says Santa. "I feel like a rock star. Maybe I'll sing a song."
"Oh, dear," says Mrs. Claus.

TODAY IS
DECEMBER
13

It's been another long day of visiting children in far-off towns and cities. Santa is just sitting down to his dinner when he gets a message from Chortle to come to the stable right away.

"*Rocketin' reindeer!*" says Santa. "What's wrong with Rudolph's nose?"

Chortle says Rudolph has a touch of the flu. It's not too serious. He just needs lots of rest and warm mash. Rudolph is feeling very sad. What if he isn't able to fly on Christmas Eve?

"Don't you worry about that!" says Santa. "It's more important that you get better."

Christmas Eve is ten days away. Chortle says all the reindeer should go to bed early every night until then.

"That's right," says Santa. "Rest up and stay healthy! If all of you get sick I'll have to go out on Christmas Eve in one of Tek's rocket-powered thingamajigs. Yikes!"

Chortle brings Rudolph extra blankets, and Santa fetches a pot of Mrs. Claus' special candy-cane tea. Then Santa sings Rudolph a lullaby to put him to sleep. It looks like his singing is working on everyone!

"Good night, everybody. Sweet dreams!"

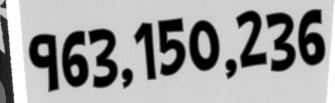

963,150,236

Santa checks in on the toy workshop. Everyone is working very hard indeed.

"Well done!" says Santa. "You're all doing a wonderful job."

"But we still have a long way to go," yelps Poppy. "Look!"

Poppy points to Tek's Terrific Toy Tabulator, which is still showing an awfully big number.

"At least we're under a billion now," says Santa.

"But what if we run out of paint? Or nails? Or stuffing?!" Poppy hops up and down in panic.

"*Hollerin' horseshoes!* We won't run out of anything," says Santa. "Everything will be fine, you'll see."

"What about that little boy, Ali? Have you decided what to take him?"

"I'm still trying to think of something," says Santa.

"Hurry up!" squeals Poppy.

"I think we both need a cup of candy-cane tea," says Santa.

TODAY IS
DECEMBER
15

Santa drops in to see Glom and Ponder, the tailor elves. He asks them to make him a new red suit because his old one is a bit tight around the middle.

"I think it shrank in the wash," he says. Glom and Ponder don't want to make the same old suit he always wears.

"Boring!" says Ponder.

"Let's try something different!" suggests Glom. "Something modern and hip."

"Yes!" says Ponder. "We'll give you a fashion makeover!"

"Uh-oh!" says Santa.

"How about some funky fringe?" asks Ponder.

"Red is so old-fashioned," says Glom. "Purple and green are trending this season."

"And patterns are all the rage," says Ponder. "We could do checks or stripes or—"

"*Thunderin' thimbles!*" says Santa. "Just make it plain, make it old-fashioned and make it red!"

The tailors agree to make the usual suit, but Ponder whispers to Glom, "Next year: polka dots!"

Santa has been doing his workout with Spark
every morning and he's enjoying it
more and more.

"*Jumpin' juniper!* I feel fantastic," he says after
a half-hour jog. "Can we keep going?"

Now he can climb all the way to the top
of the wall and ring the bell.
Ding! Ding! Ding! Ding!
"That's enough!" laughs Spark. "Now you're
just showing off!"

"Do you think I can lift that bag of toys now?" asks Santa.

"Arf arf arf!" says Puppy.

"I think that means yes," says Mrs. Claus.

"Your balance is wonderful," says Mrs. Claus.

"No more falling off the roof for me," says Santa.

Spark gives Santa top marks for improvement.

Santa is so happy he makes an announcement.

"Everyone has been working so hard, we deserve a day off tomorrow."

Hooray!

TODAY IS
DECEMBER
18

No work today! Everyone is having fun in the snow. Some elves play freeze tag, while Ember serves delicious treats. Santa is enjoying a soak in the hot tub. Tek hands him a cup of hot chocolate.

"Ahhh, thank you!" says Santa. "This is the bee's knees."

"Is a holiday really such a good idea when we have so much to do?" asks Poppy. "We'll all work better after a nice rest," says Santa.

"Have you decided on a gift for Ali yet?"

"No, but there are still six days to go," says Santa. "Relax, Poppy!"

"I won't relax until the Toy Tabulator says zero," Poppy says with a sigh.

Santa's big job today is looking over the Naughty and Nice lists. The Nice list is very long.

"So many good children!" exclaims Mrs. Claus.

Santa looks at the Naughty list and sighs. He doesn't want to leave anyone out on Christmas Eve.

"Have these children tried to be good?" he asks.

Twig reports that one girl has been reading to her little brothers at bedtime, and another boy helped his mother make supper. Other children cleaned their rooms without being asked, or donated their allowance to animal shelters, or remembered to say please and thank you.

"Put them on the Nice list!" says Santa. "Children who behave the way these children have go on the Nice list."

They spend the whole day going over these lists until the Naughty list is empty. Santa is very happy.

"Nobody really wants to be naughty," he says. "It's hard to be good all the time, but we all do our best."

"When you're done with that, it's your turn to shovel the front walk," says Mrs. Claus.

"*Blisterin' beards!*" says Santa with a frown.

"Do you want to go on the Naughty list?" asks Mrs. Claus.

Santa jumps up. "I'm going! I'm going!"

The sleigh is all ready for Christmas Eve. Tek tells Santa the new GPS screen is very easy to use. All he has to do is say "where am I?" and—*beebeep!*—the blinking yellow dot appears on the map.

"That's you," says Tek.

"Nice!" says Santa.

Just then Chortle and Rudolph walk up.

"Rudolph!" exclaims Santa. "You're looking fine and healthy, but your nose is blue."

Chortle says Rudolph is feeling much better and should be well enough to fly on Christmas Eve.

"I'm so glad," says Santa. "This gadget is pretty cool, but I still need your nose."

Tek tells them the GPS can show how far it is to the next town and if there is bad weather ahead. "And you can play tic-tac-toe on it, too."

"*Frolickin' fruitcake!*" laughs Santa. "I'm not going to have time for games." He peers closely at the screen again. "This GPS thingy will be a big help, Tek. But I still wish I could be a *red* dot."

Mrs. Claus is showing Santa the Control Room. This is where she will sit while he flies around on Christmas Eve.

"I can communicate with you all the way. I'll follow you on this map and make sure you don't miss any houses," she says.

Santa asks what all the crisscrossing lines are.

"That's your flight path," says Mrs. Claus.

Santa is shocked. "That's a long way to go." Mrs. Claus assures him it's the same route he takes every year.

"I've just never seen it on a map before," says Santa.

They are interrupted by a clucking sound. It's Tek and his Robot Chicken.

"I've found a job for the Robot Chicken," says Tek. He hands the chicken a toy truck and says, "GO!"

There's a loud whirring sound. The chicken moves so fast her wings are a blur. In just a few seconds the toy truck is beautifully wrapped.

"Ta-da!" says Tek. "A Supersonic Gift-Wrapping Chicken."

"Brilliant!" exclaims Mrs. Claus. "Poppy will be glad for the help."

"Nice job, Tek," says Santa. "Way to go!"

The loud whirring sound starts again. The chicken is wrapping Santa up!

"*Tumblin' teddy bears!*" yells Santa. "I'm not a present. Help!"

"Oops," says Tek.

TODAY IS
DECEMBER
22

The stable is buzzing with activity. Chortle grooms the reindeer, and Snippet polishes the harnesses and jingle bells until they shine.

Santa comes to check on Rudolph, who is back to full health and looking forward to flying again.

"Rudolph, my friend, you look wonderful," says Santa. "And your nose is orange, which is almost, almost red."

Just then Poppy pops in. "Santa! You haven't picked a present for Ali yet."

"I still have a couple of days left," says Santa.

"DO IT NOW!" hollers Poppy, then adds, "Please?"

"*Lords a-leapin'!* All right!" says Santa as Poppy dashes off again. Santa tells Rudolph about Ali, the lonely boy who didn't ask for anything in his letter.

"I want his gift to be very special," he sighs. "Do you think he'd like a Supersonic Gift-Wrapping Robot Chicken?"

Puppy shakes his head. He's got a better idea but he's keeping it secret for now.

Santa and Mrs. Claus watch the final toys being made. The elves are nearly done their work. They finish a doll, a Sleepy Panda, a yoyo, and a Martian toy. The toy tabulator counts down: 4 … 3 … 2 … 1 … and stops.

Everyone looks at the board in surprise. One?! There's still one gift left to make! What could it be?

Poppy turns to Santa and he blushes. "Oh yes. The present for Ali. I'm afraid I haven't—" Santa is interrupted by excited barking as Puppy jumps up on the table and picks up a bow with his teeth. Santa gets the message.

"Are you sure?" he asks. Puppy nods his head and wags his tail.

"An excellent suggestion," says Santa, with a big smile. "The perfect gift for a lonely little boy is a new puppy friend."

"Wonderful," sighs Mrs. Claus.

The Toy Tabulator clicks to zero, and everybody cheers.

"Wait, we're not done yet!" says Poppy. "There's still a lot of wrapping to do. ROBOT CHICKEN, GO!"

"*Joltin' jackrabbits!*" says Santa. "Get out of the way everyone, or she'll wrap you up, too!"

The big night has finally arrived. The sleigh is packed, and the reindeer are all in their places.

"Bravo, Rudolph!" says Santa. "There's the red nose I've been missing."

Mrs. Claus says it's time to go. Santa takes a last look at his long worklist.

"Wait!" he says. "There's one job left on my list."

"What?" squeals Poppy. "There's no time to do anything else. It's time to go."

Santa smiles. "Relax, Poppy! The last job on my list is to say thank you, everyone! You worked extra hard this year and did a spectacular job. Your presents are inside, along with a big feast. MERRY CHRISTMAS!"

The elves cheer, and Santa checks the last item off his list.

"Phew!" says Poppy.

Santa gives Mrs. Claus a kiss. "Thank you for the wool socks, dear. My toes will be toasty warm tonight."

He climbs into the sleigh. "Where am I?" he says into the GPS. *Beebeep!*

Santa stares at the screen.

"I made you a red dot," says Tek. "Merry Christmas, Santa!"

"*Twinklin' tinsel!*" laughs Santa. "Thank you, Tek."

He picks up the reins. "Reindeer, are you ready?"

The reindeer bob their heads, jingling the bells on their harnesses.

"Ho, Rudolph! Away we go!"

MERRY
CHRISTMAS,
EVERYONE!

TODAY IS
DECEMBER
25

CrackBoom! Books is an imprint of Chouette Publishing (1987) Inc.

Text: Kim Thompson
All rights reserved.
Illustrations: Élodie Duhameau

Chouette Publishing would like to thank the Government of Canada and SODEC
for their financial support.

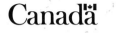

Canada

Québec ⊞⊞
Books   Gestion
Tax Credit   **SODEC**

Bibliothèque et Archives nationales du Québec and Library and Archives Canada
cataloguing in publication

Thompson, Kim, 1964-

Santa's countdown to Christmas : 24 days of stories
(CrackBoom! Books)

For children aged 3 and up.

ISBN 978-2-924786-05-5 (hardcover)

I. Duhameau, Élodie, 1983- . II. Title.

PS8639.H626S26 2017   jC813'.6   C2017-940301-X
PS9639.H626S26 2017

CRACKBOOM! BOOKS

©2017 Chouette Publishing (1987) Inc.
1001 Lenoir St., Suite B-238
Montreal, Quebec H4C 2Z6 Canada
crackboombooks.com

Printed in China
10 9 8 7 6 5 4 3 2 1   CHO2004 MAY017